7

Disney · PIXAR

TOY STORY

A Fine Feathered Friend

PaRRagon
Bath · New York · Singapore · Hong Kong · Cologne · Delhi · Melbourne

Woody the cowboy was watching TV one morning while Andy was at school. His favourite show, *Woody's Roundup*, was on. He liked to watch himself, his horse Bullseye, Jessie the cowgirl and the old Prospector rustle up some adventure in the Old West . . .

In the town of Dry Gulch, Sheriff Woody was repainting the old jailhouse. He was always looking for ways to spruce up the town.

A large drop of paint dripped off his brush. "Look out Bullseye!" Woody called to his horse.

Splat! Bullseye looked up just as the paint landed on his forehead. He whinnied.

"Sorry, fella," Woody said as he climbed down from the ladder. He pulled out his handkerchief and wiped off the paint.

Bullseye whinnied again and stomped the ground.

"Not today, partner," Woody said. "I've got to finish painting and then I'm helping Miss Tilley with her errands."

Bullseye snorted. Most mornings, he and Woody worked together. They rode out to Rattlesnake Ridge to round up cattle rustlers. Or they would patrol the town watching for bandits. But lately, it seemed like Woody was too busy to work with a partner.

Bullseye decided to find Jessie. She always had time for fun. He heard Jessie's yo-de-lay-ee-hoo as he trotted over. She was feeding peanuts to a squirrel.

"Howdy, Bullseye," she said. Bullseye walked over to Jessie. He bent his front legs so she could climb on his back.

"Oh, sorry, Bullseye," she said. "I promised to help this little guy gather some nuts for his friends. Some other time, fella."

Bullseye started walking back to town. He caught up to the Prospector, who was pushing a brand-new wheelbarrow. Bullseye whinnied.

"Hee-hee. Hello there, Bullseye," the Prospector said, chuckling.

Bullseye stopped and stomped his hoof on the ground. The Prospector usually asked Bullseye to bring his gold-mining pans down to the river. Bullseye hoped he would give him a load to carry.

But the Prospector kept walking along. "I'm gonna find me enough gold to fill this here wheelbarrow," he said.

Bullseye sadly lowered his head to munch some grass. He felt very lonely. Suddenly, he saw something sitting among the weeds. It was a brown speckled egg. Bullseye looked around for a mother hen, but there wasn't anyone in sight.

He found an old basket by the side of the road and nudged the egg inside it. Holding the handle between his teeth, he walked very slowly back to town.

"What a cute little hen's egg," Jessie said when Bullseye passed by her.

Bullseye swished his tail happily and trotted into the barn. Jessie followed him. Bullseye put down the basket and grabbed a mouthful of hay for the nest.

"It's hard work to help an egg hatch," Jessie said. "You'll have to keep it warm and watch out for snakes and raccoons. Then when the chick hatches, you'll have to care for it like its real mum. Do you think you can do it?"

Just then, Woody and the Prospector walked into the barn.

"Bullseye found an egg!" Jessie said. "He's building a nest and is going to help it hatch."

Woody smiled and patted Bullseye on the back. "That sounds like a great idea," he said.

But the Prospector wasn't so sure. "Whoever heard of a horse hatching an egg?" he said. "It's plain ol' foolishness if you ask me."

Woody pulled Jessie and the Prospector aside. "I think Bullseye's been a little lonely lately," he whispered. "This will cheer him up."

Jessie nodded. "It'll be a good thing to keep him busy," she agreed.

Bullseye cared for the egg just like a mother hen. He tucked hay around it to keep it warm. He stayed up all night to chase away raccoons and snakes. He wouldn't leave the egg for a minute.

Finally, one afternoon, Bullseye heard a tapping sound. Tap-tap-tap. It was the egg!

He watched it closely. Tap-tap-tap.

A little beak poked through the eggshell. Then – Crick! Crack! – the egg broke open!

A tiny yellow chick with spots on its back stood where the speckled egg once sat.

One afternoon, Bullseye and Horsefeathers met Woody and Jessie at the corral. Horsefeathers trotted around the ring after Bullseye. Soon the two friends started playing tag. Bullseye trotted after the little chick and touched his tail with his nose. Then Horsefeathers said, "Neigh!" and chased Bullseye until he could pull his tail with his beak.

Jessie looked worried, though. "Horsefeathers should be learning how to be a chicken, not a horse," she said quietly to Woody.

Woody rubbed his chin. "Maybe it's time to find out if Horsefeathers has a mum nearby."

Jessie watched the two friends whinny and chase each other.

Then she nodded slowly. "Maybe we should look for a mum," she said sadly. "But I haven't got the heart to do it."

Early the next morning, Horsefeathers hopped onto Bullseye's head. "Neigh!" he chirped.

Bullseye opened his eyes. It was still dark outside. But the little chick was waking up earlier and hungrier each day. Bullseye grunted. Then he got up and led Horsefeathers outside to find some breakfast.

While Bullseye chased a little green worm, Horsefeathers wandered off, pecking the dirt. A dark shadow flew over him, then circled back. When Horsefeathers looked up, he saw a hawk swooping down towards him. Horsefeathers tried to gallop away, but the hawk was gaining on him.

Suddenly, the little chick heard the sound of thundering hooves.

"Neigh!" Bullseye whinnied as the hawk flew off screeching.

Jessie and Woody ran over, having heard all the noise. Jessie scooped the little chick up in her arms. "That was close," she said to Bullseye. "You shouldn't leave Horsefeathers alone out here."

"You've done a fine job, partner," Woody told his horse. "But Horsefeathers needs to be with his real family."

Bullseye and Horsefeathers walked away.

"I didn't mean to hurt his feelings," Woody said to Jessie.

They followed Bullseye down the road. Just then, Bullseye paused to let a mother hen and her chicks pass by.

Then Woody heard the strangest sound. "Peep! Peep! Peep!"

It was Horsefeathers! For the first time, the little chick had chirped like a chicken.

Horsefeathers ran over to his mother and she tucked him under her wing. "Neigh!" Bullseye called out his good-bye.

"Neigh!" Horsefeathers chirped back. Then he walked off with his mother and brothers and sisters.

One morning, the whole gang went to visit Horsefeathers at the chicken coop. As Bullseye whinnied, a handsome rooster dashed out of the chicken house and galloped around the other birds. "That's Horsefeathers!" Jessie pointed out.

"He is one unique bird," Woody said, shaking his head.

"And Bullseye is one unique horse," Jessie added. She gave Bullseye a hug. "Good job, partner!"

Disney · PIXAR

TOY STORY

Tuned In

PaRragon

Bath · New York · Singapore · Hong Kong · Cologne · Delhi · Melbourne

Andy's toys were gathered around the TV in Andy's room. They were used to watching TV with Andy when he was home sick for a few days. The set was still pulled up next to the bed, which made it easy for the toys to turn on.

"*This* again," Bo Peep said one afternoon as a superhero show came on. "We watch this every day."

"So?" said Hamm the piggy bank. "He's the defender of the universe! What could be better? I *love* this show."

"Yeah!" agreed Rex the dinosaur. "He is one *super* hero!"

Woody the cowboy doll wasn't impressed, though. "Honestly, I don't know what Andy sees in these shows," he whispered to Buzz Lightyear the space ranger.

"Me, neither," agreed Buzz. "Call him a superhero? A few space rangers with a laser cannon could vaporize that masked man in a nanosecond, no problem."

Woody sighed and shook his head. "They just don't make TV shows like they used to," he said.

"Shows like what?" asked Buzz.

Woody grinned. "Shows like *Woody's Roundup*, of course!"

"Oh, *no*." The toys groaned. When Woody got started talking about *Woody's Roundup*, it was hard to get him to stop!

Woody's Roundup was an old show. Woody was the star –
along with Jessie the cowgirl and good old Bullseye the horse.
The show was always fresh in Woody's mind. Sometimes an
episode aired on the Western Channel, and Woody made sure to
catch it.

"Now that was a show, wasn't it?" said Woody to Jessie.

"You bet it was!" said Jessie. "Yippee hi-yi-yo!"

"Remember how it started?" Woody went on.

"You bet I do!" said Jessie. She took out her lasso and began
to twirl it. "Get over here, Bullseye!" she called.

Bullseye quickly galloped over. Then the three of them
smiled and waved to the other toys, pretending they were a
captive audience.

"Howdy, partners!" Woody hollered. "Welcome to *Woody's
Roundup!*" He jumped on Bullseye's back. "*Yeehaaah!* Giddyup!"
he cried.

While Jessie twirled her lasso and Woody and Bullseye galloped around, Rex picked up the remote control lying on Andy's pillow and pressed a button.

Suddenly, the channel changed to a *real* dinosaur show.

"Aghh!" cried Rex, diving under the covers. "Save me!" he called.

Immediately, the Green Army Men sprang into action.

"Eliminate the enemy!" Sarge ordered. "Go! Go! Go!"

One after the other, the soldiers jumped on the remote, and right away the channels began to change.

"Ooooooh!" cried one of the Aliens as the channels flew by in a blur.

"Space and time at last are one!" exclaimed another Alien.

"Perhaps this machine can help us return to our planet," they said all together.

They moved closer to the screen. "We come in peace," they told the television. "Aliens do not anger TV."

Bo Peep chuckled as she watched the Aliens. "They think they can get into the TV," she whispered to Woody. "They're so cute."

Buzz walked over to Woody. "Sheriff, I think we need to put an end to this channel surfing," he said. He pointed to the Green Army Men, who were balancing on the buttons of the remote.

Woody agreed. He was growing impatient with the flashing channels.

The flipping channels were beginning to drive the other toys crazy, too.

"Sarge, call off the troops!" Woody cried out. "I'm going to be sick from all the flashing."

"Stand down, soldiers!" Sarge commanded.

Buzz marched over to the remote control. "I'll take that," he said. Then he turned to the Aliens. "I'm sorry to break this to you, guys," he told them, "but the TV cannot return you to your planet."

The Little Green Aliens looked up to Buzz, thinking he would know how to help them get home. "Oooh," the Aliens said at the same time.

"However, the TV can take you to plenty of new places," Buzz continued. He held the remote control and carefully studied the buttons. "I know I saw a show about space somewhere back there," he declared. "All I have to do is figure out how to find it again."

"Now," said Buzz, "which button changes the channel?"

Bo Peep looked over his shoulder. "I think it's –" she began.

Buzz held up his hand. "No, no. Don't tell me," he said. "I'm good with buttons. I bet it's this one." He punched a button. But instead of changing the channel, the sound blasted from the TV. The toys all covered their ears.

"*Agghhh!*" they yelled.

Since he couldn't reach his ears to block out the noise, Rex dove under the covers again. "Save me!" he cried.

"What did I do?" asked Buzz. He dropped the remote on the bed.

Bo Peep carefully reached around him with her staff and gently turned down the volume.

Buzz sighed with relief. "Thanks, Bo," he said.

"Enough playing around, already," Hamm said. "Let's turn back to the superheroes before Andy gets back."

"But we can watch that show anytime," Slinky Dog complained. "I think we should watch the Animal Channel instead."

This started all the toys thinking about their favourite shows. They couldn't decide what to watch!

"I'd like to watch the Fairy Tale Channel," said Bo Peep.

"How about the Military Channel?" said Sarge.

"Or the Cooking Channel!" said Rex.

"Or the Cowboy Channel!" said Jessie. "We can watch a real-live rodeo!"

"Well, I guess there's just one way to decide what to watch," Hamm declared.

"How?" asked Rex.

"Ask the TV?" said the Aliens.

"No," Hamm said. "We'll take a vote."

"Huh?" said Woody. "I didn't say anything."

"Well, would you look at that!" said Jessie, "Woody and I are on TV!" The Cowboy Channel was showing an episode of *Woody's Roundup*!

"Now *there's* a show!" said Woody.

And everyone else had to agree!